Harry Potter

AND THE ORDER OF THE PHOENIX

Movie Poster Book

SCHOLASTIC INC.

NEW YORK   TORONTO   LONDON   AUCKLAND   SYDNEY
MEXICO CITY   NEW DELHI   HONG KONG   BUENOS AIRES

ISBN-13: 978-0-439-02491-4
ISBN-10: 0-439-02491-9
Copyright © 2007 by Warner Bros. Entertainment Inc.
HARRY POTTER characters, names, and related indicia are trademarks of and © Warner Bros. Entertainment Inc.
Harry Potter Publishing Rights © JKR.
(s07)

12 11 10 9 8 7 6 5 4 3 2 1   7 8 9 10 11/0
Printed in the U.S.A.

First printing, June 2007

HARRY POTTER

HERMIONE GRANGER

RON WEASLEY

FRED AND GEORGE WEASLEY

DRACO MALFOY

GINNY WEASLEY

PADMA PATIL

CHO CHANG

GREGORY GOYLE

VINCENT CRABBE

NEVILLE LONGBOTTOM

LUNA LOVEGOOD

NYMPHADORA TONKS